Why Daddy Bear Is Having Surgery

A Child's View of Open Heart Surgery

Jennifer Bonnell

Illustrated by Carlos Báez

ISBN:1505520223
ISBN-13:9781505520224

DEDICATION

This book is dedicated to my stepfather Robert Hunt who has had two open heart surgeries and has safely recovered from both.

ACKNOWLEDGMENTS

I would like to thank Carlos Báez for illustrating my book,
Deb Jacobs for working with me through this whole process,
and my mother Sandy Hunt for giving up countless
hours of her time to help me complete this project.

Hello there! My name is Hank. I'm going to tell you a story about Daddy Bear.

This is Daddy Bear, his chest has been hurting lately.

Daddy Bear has had trouble playing around and is tired more often. Everyone is starting to notice.

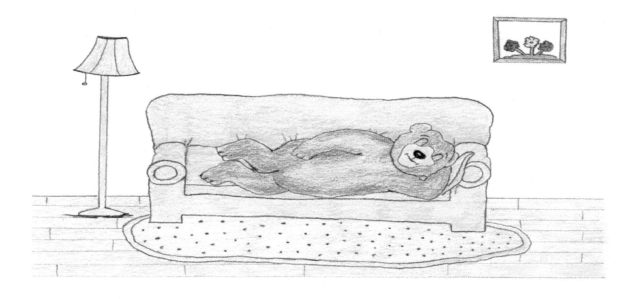

3

Mama Bear suggests he visit the doctor.

4

Mama Bear explains to the children that Daddy Bear is going for a checkup.

The next day Mama and Daddy Bear go to the doctor's office for his appointment.

The doctor says everything looks good on the outside, but he is displaying symptoms of heart disease and needs to get a few tests done.

 The doctor comes back to tell Mama and Daddy Bear that Daddy Bear has heart disease. The doctor then schedules Daddy Bear to have open heart surgery.

The two most common types of heart surgery are Bypass surgery and Stent Implants.

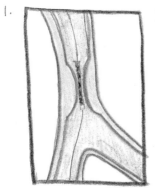

• Stent goes into artery

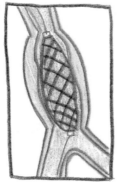

• Stent gets inflated

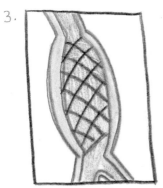

• Stent stays in place to hold artery open

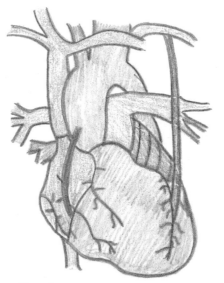

• the bypass goes over the clogged artery

Stents

Bypass

The doctor explains to Daddy and Mama Bear that they are going to do Bypass surgery.

The next day, everyone comes to the hospital with Daddy Bear because they love him.

The doctor explains to the children what heart disease is.

Heart Disease is the most common disease in America. It is caused by plaque buildup which stiffens artery walls and limits blood flow throughout your body. Plaque buildup can be caused by smoking, poor diet, and not exercising. Heart disease can also be passed down from parents and even grandparents.

The nurses prep Daddy Bear for surgery and take him back to the operating room.

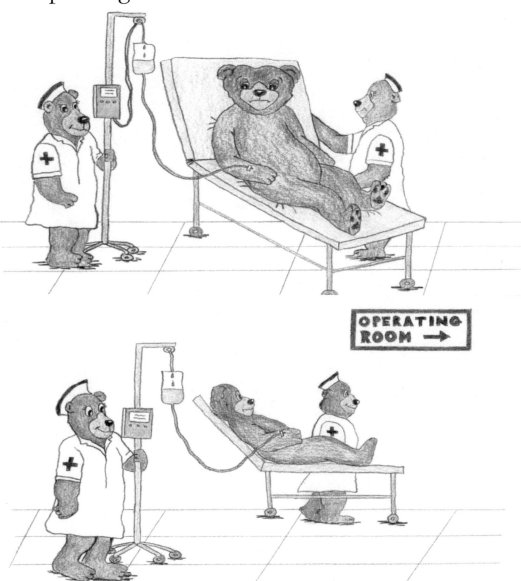

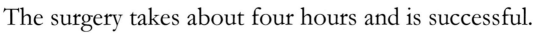

The surgery takes about four hours and is successful.

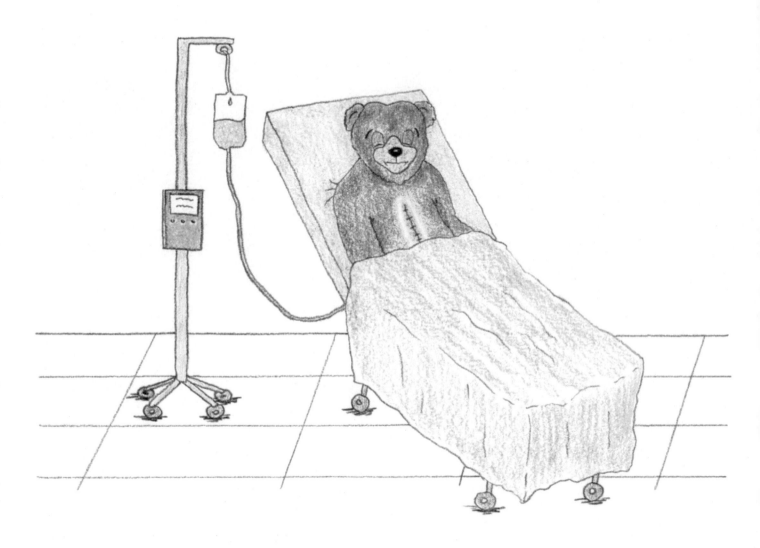

 Daddy Bear is taken back to his room to make sure he recovers well after the surgery.

 After a couple of days, Daddy Bear is ready to come home.

NO SMOKING

 Daddy Bear comes home from the hospital and has to make some lifestyle changes.

 Daddy Bear needs to take daily medicines in order to stay healthy.

 Healthy eating and exercising can help Daddy Bear live a long and healthy life.

ABOUT THE AUTHOR

Jennifer Bonnell attends Deep Creek High School's Science and Medicine Academy. She is also a varsity field hockey and soccer player, and a Girl Scout Ambassador. Jennifer graduates in June 2015. She plans on attending a four year college after high school in order to receive a degree in athletic training. This book represents the culminating achievement of her
Girl Scout Gold Award project.

Made in United States
Orlando, FL
22 May 2022

18072709R00015